To Number 1326 of the

Connecticut Trolley Museum —

my inspiration for this story

and to my family for their support.

by Rachel Stewart Spector

Illustrated by Susan L. Schadt

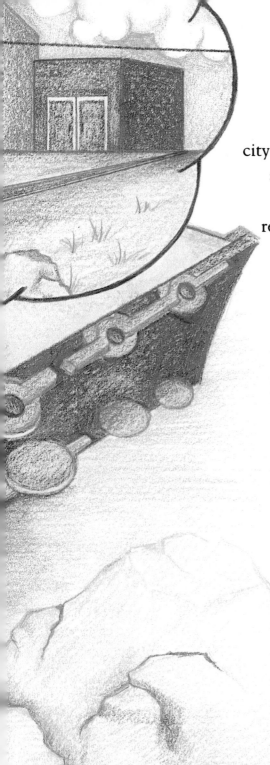

Tilley the Trolley woke up from a wonderful dream.

She dreamed that she was back in the city of Waterbury busily shuffling people to and from work at the factories. She was loaded with 200 passengers, some reading newspapers, others talking about work, their families or local events.

Tilley especially liked it when certain newspaper headlines would have everyone talking. She learned so much about the world and people in far away places. Some of the news seemed to make the passengers very happy, and sometimes it made them sad or angry. She loved learning about the world, and she loved being around people. She was so happy. "Who could have a better life than this?" thought Tilley.

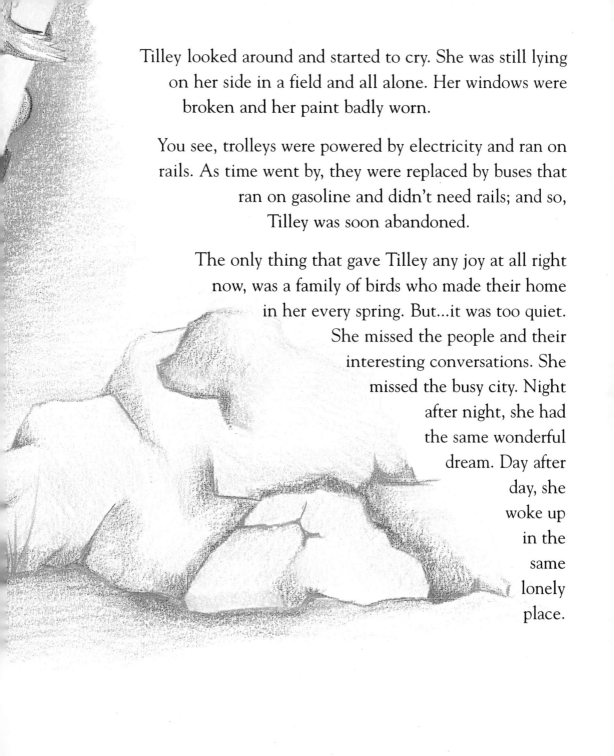

Tilley looked around and started to cry. She was still lying on her side in a field and all alone. Her windows were broken and her paint badly worn.

You see, trolleys were powered by electricity and ran on rails. As time went by, they were replaced by buses that ran on gasoline and didn't need rails; and so, Tilley was soon abandoned.

The only thing that gave Tilley any joy at all right now, was a family of birds who made their home in her every spring. But...it was too quiet. She missed the people and their interesting conversations. She missed the busy city. Night after night, she had the same wonderful dream. Day after day, she woke up in the same lonely place.

One day, after a long nap, Tilley woke up
and heard someone crying. A boy named
Billy, who loved to go exploring on his own,
had lost his compass through a hole in his pocket.
"Now I'll never figure out the way home," cried Billy. "I shouldn't have
wandered so far. I have no idea where I am. Without my compass, I am
truly lost!" Then, he said to Tilley, "I wish you could take me home, but
you look like you've been lost for a very long time. It must have been
fun riding a trolley," thought Billy.

He was tired, and
decided to sit down
under the weeping willow tree that was near Tilley.
He started to yawn and soon fell asleep. Tilley wanted
to help, "but what could a broken-down old trolley do?"
she thought sadly. She couldn't even "toot" to alert anybody.
She thought back to the days when she had passengers and how special their
children seemed to be to them. They would talk about their children with such
love and pride. Tilley was sure someone would come looking for Billy soon.

A couple of hours passed, and sure enough, Tilley heard voices. Billy woke up and heard his name being called. "Over here!" he shouted. Billy saw his family, neighbors and even some firemen. He explained to them how he had lost his compass. Everyone was just grateful that he was all right.

One of the firemen looked over at Tilley. He said, "My folks used to tell me that to get anywhere in the city, they would ride a trolley. After a long day at work, my father would board the trolley, close his eyes, and the gentle motion and rhythmic sounds would sometimes rock him to sleep. He said that it was such a delightful way to travel."

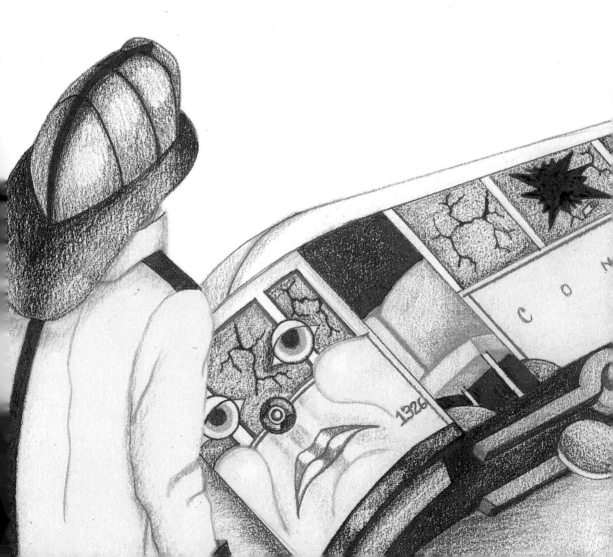

Looking again at Tilley and shaking his head, he said, "What a shame...what a shame." Before he turned to leave, he got a twinkle in his eye. "Maybe it's not too late for you old girl," he said, as he walked away.

Early the next morning, Tilley was awakened by men calling out orders. She soon found herself being jacked up and put on a flatbed truck. As the truck drove off, she worried, "What is going on and where are they taking me?"

After a while, Tilley forgot her worries and
started to enjoy the ride. She looked all around as
the truck moved along. "Roads are wider with many lanes and
automobiles are bigger and faster. There are so many of them, too, in
all kinds of colors. My how things have changed." Tilley thought to
herself. Back in the days when Tilley was in the city, there were very
few cars and most all of them were black.

Tilley was so lost in her thoughts, that she didn't realize the truck had stopped. She wasn't in the city, but she was in a place where there were other trolleys! She was pleased but rather puzzled.

Soon she was removed from the truck and placed in a barn. Many people got busy fixing her up. There were men and women replacing windows. They cleaned and repaired her beautiful cane seats and replaced all of her wood that had become rotten. Tilley got five coats of paint in her original bright colors. She was yellow, which seemed to glow as bright as the sun, and her fiery red letters and trim made her stand out all the more.

Tilley had no idea how much time had passed. She did know that she was fussed over day and night for a very long time, and now she felt as good as new.

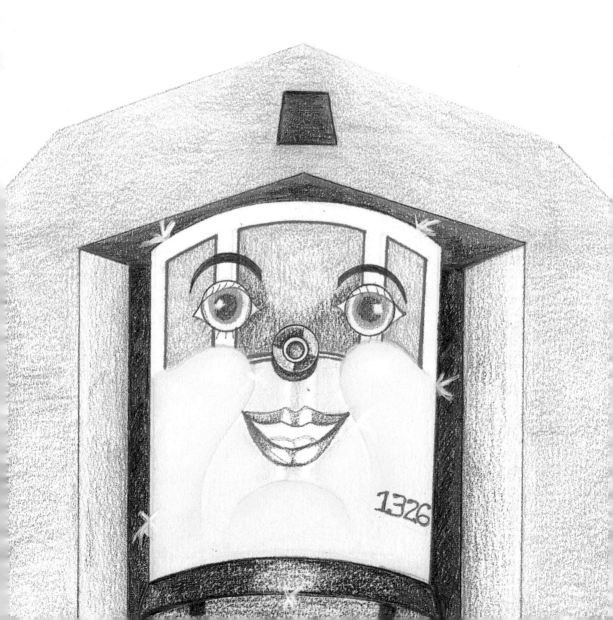

The other trolleys seemed to be very busy. Tilley constantly heard their whistles blowing and their wheels humming on the rails. She couldn't understand why so many people drove their automobiles to a big lot and parked, only to board a trolley. Also, the trolleys returned to the same spot with the same people!

"I'm so confused," thought Tilley.

Then finally, one day, she heard a little girl say, "Can we come back to the trolley museum soon Daddy?"

"So...that's where I am — a museum for trolleys!" exclaimed Tilley. Tilley was very impressed because, in the city, her passengers often talked about museums and how wonderful they were.

Later that day, two of the museum workers came over to Tilley. One man said to the other, "We've had a lot of telephone calls asking for birthday parties here. What should we do?"

The other man replied, "I think Tilley would make a great Birthday Trolley. She's colorful, and, unlike the other trolleys, she has two long seats on either side. We could set up tables between them." "Birthday Trolley"...Tilley liked the sound of that. "But, what was a birthday?" she wondered.

HAPPY BIRTHDAY ! ! !

Tilley became the Birthday Trolley, and she soon found out that birthdays meant lots of cake, lots of singing, and lots of happy children. She enjoyed her new job, even though it was quite different from her city job. She learned to love the children and their parties, and always let them blow her whistle before the party was over.

"Who could have a better life than this?" thought Tilley. Then she blew a "toot toot" from her whistle that all was well.